I0675811

Forgotten Lies

Michael A. Young

ROYAL MEDIA
AND PUBLISHING LLC

Royal Media and Publishing
P. O. Box 4321
Jeffersonville, IN 47131
502-802-5385
http://royamediaandpublishing.com
royalmediapublishing@gmail.com

© Copyright – 2020

All Rights Reserved.   No part of this book may be reproduced, stored in a retrieval system, or transmitted by any means without the written permission of the author.

Cover Design: Gad of Elite Book Covers

ISBN-13: 978-0-9987154-8-3

Printed in the United States of America

Table of Contents

Prologue

The smell of burning oak and burnt hickory filled the air. Hundreds of leaves scattered as a small SUV followed by a moving truck cruised through the countryside. A family of three were relocating to a quiet country town very far from hustle and bustle of the city life. Even though it was considered country, this town wasn't country per se. No big farms or tractors driving down the main road of town. This was just a small town. Much like any small town, you would pull off the expressway to fill up at a gas station. No large towers of glass. No stopping at a busy intersection every 50 feet. This was a place where ordinary folk could get an ordinary job to support their family and be completely happy doing so. No stress of trying to move up the corporate ladder. No worry of making financial reports or timelines.

About 20 minutes after entering the town, the SUV pulled up to a house that sat in the middle of a field surrounded by large trees. The two-story home looked like a painting, in part because of the beautiful autumn leaves that still hung from the trees and those lying on the ground. The home had a long gravel driveway that led to the paved road. This wasn't the only house around, but the neighbors' homes were well off at a distance. This land used to be farmlands, but as more factories opened up in the town, more and more farmers had turned into industrial workers. Those who refused to do anything but farm, were moving further and further out. So, homes like this were becoming available to those willing to move away from city life.

The doors opened on the vehicle, and a man stepped out and put his hands on his hips. Then a woman stepped out of the passenger side and opened the back door to let a very young boy out of his car seat. The boy was no older than four or five. Immediately he took off running through the leaves and around the trees. The woman went over to the man and was embraced in a hug. He kissed her on the forehead and asked, "Are you sure you're ready for this life?"

She answered with a smile, "More important, are you ready for this life? Because I'll follow you anywhere that will make you happy."

As the man leaned down to kiss his lady, the moving men exited their van. Also, at that moment, a pickup truck came down the driveway. The truck belonged to Sarah Plack, the realtor that sold the home. She gave a kind hello to the moving men and they replied hello in the same manner.

"Mr. and Mrs. Tonner. How was your trip here from the city?"

Mr. Tonner answered, "Besides a flat tire on the van, the journey down was rather pleasant. The fresh air is a refreshing change. After years of breathing car fumes and other exhausts, the smell of wood on a fire is more than welcomed."

"That's right honey. This is a change we both needed. I mean all three of us needed.

Clint will love all the room he has to roam around in now," Cindy Tonner said.

"That is so reassuring. Patrick mentioned you both would love a house with plenty of land, but not too far from the factory," Sarah said with a big smile as she fished for the keys to the house in her briefcase.

Patrick went over to the movers and let them know that they could start unloading the van shortly. He looked over his shoulder to see the two women walking to the front door and noticed his son had found a tire swing hanging from a tree limb. Mr. Tonner moved quickly to the SUV and opened the hatchback. Removing a cooler, he ran back to the back of the moving van and tossed a can of beer to each mover. The three men all cracked their cans open as they sat on the lift.

"Drink up men. Two women looking around a new house! We got time to put a serious dent in this 12-pack we have here," Patrick stated as all three men held up their beers and then drank.

Cindy and Sarah walked into the house. As soon as Cindy saw the inside of the home, a giant smile went across her face. Then she was struck with a massive headache. The pain in her head was so intense that it made her lose her balance and lean against a wall. Very concerned, Sarah ran over to her and asked if she was alright and if she needed to yell for her husband.

Cindy said, "No, no! I'll be fine. I just got a headache from somewhere. Must be exhausted from the move and trip down here. Please continue showing me around."

After helping Mrs. Tonner up, they continued to walk around looking at the house. Sarah began walking arm-in-arm with Cindy. This was to come off as being friendly and having a personal interest in her clients' happiness in the home. Also, it was to make sure Mrs. Tonner didn't have another loss of balance again. After a few moments Sarah felt confident Cindy was OK, and she released her arm and walked in front of her pointing out special perks of the house like views from windows, closet space, and spaciousness.

Pausing to look at a window, Cindy saw a rope swing from a big limb on a big tree in the field. As she tried to focus on the rope, another headache struck her. Then she saw something swinging from the rope. Her eyes strained through the head pain and she saw a body swinging from the bottom of the rope. A boy. A little boy. Hanging from the rope. Cindy yells, "Clint! Clint! Patrick, oh my God, go help Clint!"

Hearing his wife yell his son's name along with frantic cries for help, Patrick dropped his beer and took off running to where his son was playing. The two movers also let their drinks go to see if the man needed their help.

Patrick ran to his son swinging and laughing on the tire swing. The movers stopped running right behind him. Cindy came running from around the corner, crying and calling the boy's name.

Hearing his name in a way that wasn't good the boy stopped swinging and got off the rope. Cindy ran up to him and grabbed him looking the boy over.

Patrick asks, "What was wrong with what he was doing? Your yelling scared the shit out of me!"

Wiping away tears she explained that from her viewpoint in the house upstairs, it looked like Clint was hanging from the rope, not swinging on it.

Patrick said, "Holy shit, woman!" Then he smiled as he rubbed his sons head then hugged his wife.

Cindy glanced back up at the window, and another pain shot through her head, and she saw a faint shadowy form of a person looking down on them. Still looking up, she said, "I bet I scared the hell out of our realtor too." Just then Sarah Plack came from around the side of the house holding her heels in her hand.

"Is everything OK? I heard Mrs. Tonner yelling.

Seeing Sarah outside, Cindy had a puzzled look on her face. Then she looked back up at the window to see that the figure was gone. No way Sarah could have been up there and gotten outside that fast. So who was it that she saw in the window? Or did see even see anyone up there at all?

The group walked back around to the front of the house. It took a couple hours, but everything in the van was now in the house and in rooms. Sarah Plack left shortly after they came back to the front. Waving goodbye to the movers as they pulled away, the Tonners turned to go into their new home together. Then a cold chill ran up Cindy's back as she looked at the house. "What the

hell is going on with me all of a sudden,"
Cindy thought to herself.

Chapter I

After about a week, the Tonners were settled into their new home. Patrick felt comfortable in the plant. Young Clint had started school and was doing OK. Cindy was still having headaches. They were so bad that Cindy had decided to make a trip back to the city to see her longtime doctor. As she returned home, pulling into the driveway, she saw a figure moving around between the trees. Figuring it was Sarah Plack checking on them or perhaps a neighbor coming to introduce themselves, she parked her car that she got out of storage during her visit to the city and walked over towards the visitor. As she got closer the figure began to fade, but at the same time it was walking towards her.

Stopping to rub her eyes and blink, thinking the sun is playing tricks on her, Cindy stood still waiting for her eyes to refocus. After her eyes focused, the figure no longer could be seen. Looking around confused, she tried to make sense of what she saw or thought she saw. Then suddenly the figure rushed at her just a few feet away. Startled, Cindy fell backward and let off a scream. Sitting on the ground and looking up, she saw no one anywhere. Flipping over and looking side to side, she said, "What the hell? I know someone was just in my fucking face, or something was, dammit!" She dusted herself off. Goosebumps covered her arms along with leaves and twigs. Cindy went into the house and began to fix a snack for Clint when he got home from school and make plans for dinner when Patrick came home.

After they finished dinner and the dishes were washed, they both put Clint to bed and kissed him good night. With the young boy sleepy and in bed, the couple curled up together to watch a horror movie that Patrick had been wanting to see. Cindy didn't particularly like those kind of movies, but she would suffer through them to please her guy. She did a lot of things like that for Patrick. He wanted a bigger family, but she was unable to give him any kids. Clint was his son from a previous relationship. Patrick knew Cindy couldn't give him more kids from the beginning. She told him of the accident she was in that claimed the life of her parents and older brother. His love for her was so strong, the fact he couldn't have any more natural kids didn't bother him. He wanted and needed Cindy in his life and his son's life. Thanks to her doctor Chris Hoss, Cindy was able to recover and lead a halfway normal life. After several surgeries and therapies, she recovered. So since then, Dr. Hoss had been the only doctor she would see. He knew everything about her.

It was late and the scream flick was finally over. Feeling scared, but slightly turned on from the out of place sex scenes in the movie, Cindy bit on Patrick's ear, then pulled her pants down as she headed up the stairs.

Kissing, touching, and rubbing, the time was right. Cindy whispered, "Get the lube, baby." He said, "I think we left it downstairs."

She laid back and seductively said, "You know, no slipping and sliding if the ride ain't wet."

Smiling, he jumped out of bed and went downstairs looking for lube. Cindy got up and went into the walk-in closet. Feeling a little freaky, she searched for some playthings. To watch the movie, he fixed her a little cocktail to relax her, and the drink had worked its magic between her legs. As she continued to look the lights went off in the room.

"Oh, I see you must be ready to get wet and wild." She turned and saw a man standing in the room. After saying some naughty things but getting no response, she said, "What are you doing, Pat? We're not role-playing horror scenes in here." Then the man's eyes began to glow as he moved towards her. She screamed and ran to the bathroom and closed the door. Patrick ran back upstairs and into the room. Calling Cindy's name, he knocked on the bathroom door.

She answered through the door, "Someone was in here! He turned out the lights and came at me and his eyes were glowing, Pat! His fucking eyes were glowing!"

"Cin! There is no one here. I was at the bottom of the steps looking for the lube, heard you scream and ran back. No way in hell someone passed by me. Going either way. Up or down. Plus, the lights in the room were on. Been on. I could see them on down there."

"Are you sure Pat? I thought it was you, but you didn't answer me. Plus, his eyes. His eyes looked like they glowed!"

Finally calming Cindy down, the mood was ruined. He made a check throughout the house, checking locks and windows only after he went and looked in on Clint. Satisfied no one was in the house, Cindy drifted off to sleep in Patrick's arms, but before her mind replayed the figure walking by the trees and in her room. It was the same figure. The eyes. The glowing eyes.

Chapter II

Patrick sat at work with his mind in a cloud. Eyes closed, head leaning back, and hands folded behind his head. Very concerned about his wife, he wondered if this move for this job was really best for this family. True enough the pay was good. Shit, the pay was outstanding! The work he did for the company back at the plant in the city was much more difficult. Patrick didn't mind getting his hands dirty. Matter of fact, he didn't mind helping anyone out, but being left to complete someone else's work was what he hated. Much too often, that was the case in the city. Patrick was an engineer for a rising truck company. A combined effort by German technology, Italian design, and

American toughness. In no way did this automotive trinity think they would be knocking any of the major brands out of place. Their only objective was to make a quality product that consumers would like. Since a lot of the work was done by actual workers and not by machines, there was a constant demand for engineering to be present. With quality training and something that was almost unheard of in factory production. The factory management actually listened to the workers. Who better knew when something was wrong or would work better than the people building the product. Pat was hired to be the rep engineer for the company that spoke and worked with the work force rep.

Here at the truck plant, Pat had been called to the floor numerous times, but with good communication with the other rep, the issues were addressed and handled with ease and speed. So, in this first week, it felt like all the stress from the last four years in the city plant were falling off every second. The only stress he felt here was the current problems his wife was having. The headaches and seeing figures were really bothering him. The only thing keeping him from staying at home every day with her was that she said her doctor said it was just stress and nerves from going to a different environment and lifestyle. Dr. Chris Hoss said it may take up to a month to adjust completely, and if the issues continued after that, he would set her up with a psychiatrist. Cindy said Dr. Hoss didn't like to prescribe drugs unless it was a medical condition.

The phone rang, snapping him out of his lull. With what was going through his mind, he automatically thought it was Cindy. Grabbing the phone on his desk he slowly picks up the receiver and said, "Hello??? Tonner."

The voice on the other end says, "Mr. Tonner. It's me again. There is a problem with an air gun on the frame line. It's under torquing. The worker says he think there may be an air leak in the hose somewhere."

"OK Joe. I'm on the way down. Put one of the medical extras on a torque wrench until we get the gun issue solved."

"Will do. See you shortly." Joe answered then hung up.

Relived it was a work call, Patrick got out of his chair and headed out of his office. Just as he got in his in-plant cart, his cell phone vibrated. Pulling the phone out and swiping the unlock, he saw he had a text message. A message from Cindy. He let out a breath of exhaustion. Saying to himself, "Please let everything be alright."

The text read, "I hope you are having another wonderful day. I was just thinking of you while I was waiting for Clint to come home. I love you. By the way, could you bring home some bread and paper towels?

With a smile of relief, he responded, "Sure thing, Cin. See you when I get off." Putting the phone back in his pocket, he rolled away ready to do his job with his mind a little clearer.

Chapter III

After a month in their new home, the Tonners had settled in. Finally. Patrick loved his job, and Clint was doing well in head start. Cindy had even found a part-time job in town. For a couple hours a day and every other Saturday, she worked at City Hall in the records department. The work was kind of taxing on her, but it did help occupy her mind and time. Her headaches had even subsided slightly. The visions of the figure didn't come to her as much, but they still came. The figure never came close to her again. It just stayed off at a distance. Sort of watching her. To keep Patrick from worrying so much she didn't tell him every time she saw...it. Just every now and then.

The couple even got to know the neighbors close to them. Though they weren't really close in distance, they were close enough for visits. The closest family was the Bocks, an elderly couple that lived on their right side. The Bocks had lived there in the same home for over 30 years. Terry Bock was a retired police officer. Samantha Bock was a retired school teacher. Sometimes she would still stop by the elementary and middle schools to help out with special events. She was still very well loved.

The Bocks started coming by about a week after the Tonners moved in. Said they wanted to wait till they settled in before coming by. The older couple was great to talk to. They would spend hours on each other's decks discussing the differences in city and small-town life. Mr. Bock would get so excited that most times he would raise up out of his seat to make his point. He never did this in anger. Just overly enthused to prove his point. Most of the time he would win because his verbal sparring partner would be laughing too hard to continue.

On the left side lived Lamont and Elizabeth Huff. The Huffs were a younger couple that moved in about a year before the Tonners. The Huffs were a fun-loving couple. Adventure junkies is another commonly used term. The two had been skydiving, deep sea diving, on a safari in Africa, and, most recently, they had spent their vacation in Spain at the running of the bulls. Lamont was almost gored, and Elizabeth had a few cracked ribs from being run over by a smaller bull. Both said it was the most thrilling moments of their lives. Now they lived here in this quiet country town because a very good friend of theirs had died while cliff jumping in Hawaii. "Damn fool," Lamont called his friend. Damn fool. After his death Elizabeth said she couldn't bear to hear any news about Mont dying or him receiving news of her death. So they had moved here and calmed down. Now the most they did was water ski, jet ski, or take hot air balloon rides.

It was a dark country night, but the sky was clear and filled with stars. The stars looked like flashing lights way off in the distance. A warm breeze flowed through the small country area. With the warm air and the smell of the different trees mixed with burning wood in fire pits, it was a perfect night for sitting outside and enjoying it.

The Tonners, the Huffs, and the Bocks sat on the back deck of the Tonners' home. Patrick and Lamont had double-teamed the grill while Terry sat back in a chair and gave grilling instructions as he downed a couple beers. Every now and then, he would get up during a conversation to symbolize the proof in what he was saying, and also to tell the guys to turn whatever was on the grill at that time. Terry Bock was so funny and so fun to have around, they would just humor him by doing as instructed or disagree to make him get even louder and more animated.

Inside the women fixed side dishes for the cookout and had a little private girl talk. They discussed their husbands, jobs, and their lives before moving here. The Tonners were new to the county. The Huffs were still kind of new, but had settled in very quickly. The Bocks had lived there the longest. They knew a lot about the area.

"Most of these homes are really old. Especially your house Cindy. With an added bonus, there was a vicious murder committed here. A neighboring couple was killed and a young boy was also killed. I don't know all the details, but I'm sure Terry does," Samantha told the women while sipping a glass of wine.

Cindy and Elizabeth looked at each other wide-eyed and with their mouths dropped open. The two yelled, "TERRY!!!!" at the same time. Rushing out the door they called and ran at Terry talking over each other.

He was in the middle of explaining another point to the guys. When the sound of his name was yelled out, he dropped his drink and almost fell out of the chair he was in. He said, "What the hell!?" with a surprised look on his face.

The ladies came out to him, pulled him up out of his scat, and asked him to tell them about the former residents of their homes. Dusting himself off, he said, "Alright,

alright, I'll tell you. Let me calm my nerves and get a fresh beer."

Patrick reached over into the cooler, pulled a cold beer out, and tossed it over to Terry. For a man his age, his reflexes were still very good. Cracking open the can, he sat back down and announced, "Gather round, kiddies, and let me tell you a tail of sadness, madness, murder, and lost souls. Let me tell you a story about a man named Jed. A poor mountaineer that barely kept his family fed..."

Lamont grabbed some ice and threw it at Terry. "This ain't the Beverly Hillbillies, you damn fool!!!"

Laughing so hard he had tears in his eyes, Terry said, "OK, OK, I'm done playing. Truthfully, there was a death here in this house. Possibly more, but for sure at least one. A neighbor. From your home, actually, Lamont. Ya see, the family here was the Dentons, Max and Vivian Denton. They had three kids. Candice, the oldest girl, at 10 years old. Her 8-year-old brother, Christopher, and their baby sister, Krissy. The details were never really explained, but we were told that Max and Vivian were having a huge argument, and a neighbor, Big Fred, from your home Lamont, came by to borrow something or other and heard the two inside. He ended up dead along with Max. Supposedly Vivian left with the kids and had an accident on a sharp curve going through the woods about four miles down the road.

Her car was found burnt up due to the accident."

"Oh my God, that's terrible!" Cindy said, covering her mouth.

Elizabeth went over and held Lamont's hand, and he took a big swallow of the beer he was drinking.

"Were the kids killed in the accident too?" Patrick asked.

"There were only two bodies found in the car. Burnt. The town's best guest was that the girl survived somehow and wandered into the woods, but a kid that small and young couldn't have possibly survived. Sadly, and more than likely, one of the forest animals found her and....."

Now the men teared up. Even Terry got watery-eyed telling the story. "That is the main reason the woods were cleared out. People hoped against all hope that she was still out there somewhere, or at least her body would be recovered."

Samantha said, "OK, Terry, the mood here has gotten too heavy. We need to liven things up again. Will you go in and get the strawberry pies I made?"

"Sure thing, honey," Terry answered. Then he stopped and looked at the guys. "You go get the dessert. That's woman's work. Us men need to make sure this meat is done and the fire is out."

Lamont looks over at Patrick and repeats, "Us?!" They both laughed and were joined by Terry in the laughter, realizing he had been called out on his so-called help.

"Come on ladies, let's let these cavemen take care of their business," Samantha said as she tagged Terry in the back of the head walking past him.

Once the ladies finished preparing a dessert that would go along with the fellows' beer, their wine, and the bags of chips and wedges of cheese, they headed back outside. By now, the air was cooler. Patrick lit torches around the deck for light, warmth, and to keep bugs away for the time being.

As Cindy was about to join everyone on the deck, her nose was filled with the smell of something burning. As she turned to the stove she saw the flickering glow of the oven like something might still be inside and burning. She quickly moved toward it when she stopped dead in her tracks. The....door....was moving. Like whatever was inside was trying to get out. Cindy took slow steps and stopped directly in front of it. Then when she bent down and looked closer, a burning hand smacked the glass of the oven door. A face slammed against it next. The face of Clint. He was in the oven and burning!!!!!

Cindy let out a bone-chilling scream. Then yelled, "Clint, no!!!!!! Patrick, help!! Clint is in there burning!!!! Patrick, help!!!!!!"

Patrick jumped up, followed by everyone else. Even Terry was moving like a younger man. Fear and danger can have that effect. Especially when a child is in danger. They all ran into the kitchen to find Cindy on the floor in front of the oven. Pulling on the door crying. Patrick kneeled down next to her with hands shaking. He asked her, "Cin, what's wrong? Where's Clint? What's wrong with him? Cin, talk to me!"

Looking at him through watery eyes, she said, "Don't you see him? He's in there! He's burning!"

"In where, Cin?"

"There! In the oven! He's burning. He's burning!"

Patrick looked at the oven, then at Cindy. "Honey! Clint's not in there. The oven isn't even on. Look. Cold as the kitchen floor."

Cindy shook her head no, then looked at the stove. It was off. Had been off for hours. Just at that moment, Clint walked in dragging his pillow. He had done his usual routine. Fallen asleep in the living room watching cartoons. Cindy looked at Patrick, then everyone else, and said she swore she saw him in there. As she began sobbing again, Patrick just held her and feared she might be losing her mind.

Chapter IV

Samantha stepped out of the hall into the den where Terry was. He stood in front of a big cabinet filled with collectable die-cast cars of different sizes. Terry held a beer can in his hand and would raise it to take a drink, but then lower it every time without drinking. Samantha watched him in the doorway for a few moments, then asked him if he was alright.

"Yeah, Sammy, I'm fine. Just having one more beer before bed."

"That wouldn't be a problem if you were actually drinking it. I've watched you raise and lower that can for the last 10 minutes.

Terry, you can drink a beer in a single breath. What is on your mind, dear?"

Terry looked at the can, then placed it on a small table near the cabinet. He turned to look at his wife. He looked at her face, aging but still beautiful. She had been by his side through the best moments in his life and also some of his worst. With sad eyes he looked at her and said, "I'll be fine, Sammy, I'm OK."

"Bullshit, Terry. You telling everybody about what happened in the Tonners home shook you up a little, baby, and that's fine to say. It was a horrible thing that happened. There's not many left that know even that much of that story."

She turned to go back down the hall and spoke over her shoulder to him. "By the way, why didn't you tell them everything that happened and what you found in the woods?"

"Sammy, the Tonners are young and new to the area. I didn't want to be the reason they couldn't sleep anymore. They don't need to know everything that happened. Lamont and Elizabeth are too much of...too much. They are the type to go looking and digging until they find something...anything."

Terry went to his den and sat in his comfy chair. Picking up the remote, he pointed it at the TV in the corner. Instead of turning it on, he just stared at the black screen. His hand trembled slightly. Because on the dark screen his mind was playing what really happened that horrible night in the woods. The car, smashed into a tree with smoke coming from the motor. The blood-soaked interior, with the dead body hanging out of the driver's side window, being chewed on by a couple of wolves. There were a few dead wolves lying about. Also there were...pieces of meat scattered around. Possibly the remains of the little girl whose body was never found. Especially since it took the other cops so long to get there.

Terry was first on the scene because he was on the way home, having just gotten off duty. He heard the faint sound of screams, and he heard the sound of a car crash. In all his years on the force, never had he seen so much blood. Bodies, yes, but never fresh bodies in this shape. Even after all that. One thing that really bothered him was what was found back at the family's home. It was something directly out of a Hollywood horror movie. That poor family. What happened in that house? The house where the Tonners lived now.

Lost in his thoughts, Terry was startled by Samantha's hand touching his shoulder. His arm finally lowered with remote in hand as he looked at his wife with a pale face. She kneeled next to him with concern in her eyes. Seeing natural fear in her face, his love for her pumped blood back in his face. He took her hand and stood, helping her to her feet also.

"I'm fine, Sammy. Just an old man fighting sleep like a young baby, and just like that baby, this old man is losing to sleep. Come on honey, let's turn in. I've had my fill of beers tonight. Time to rest these old bones. Never know what I may have to teach these young people tomorrow."

"Teach. You got that right, you old dog. You sure won't be showing no one how to do anything," Samantha said as she took her hand from his and started to walk away.

"I can still show you a few things," Terry said, swatting her on her bottom.

Chapter V

An SUV sat on the side of the road right in the middle of Gideon Forest. To see some kind of vehicle sitting off road around this way wasn't that unusual. You could find hikers, campers, or mountain bikers in the forest at any moment. This particular part of the forest hadn't been a very popular area since that time the remains of that family were found nearby. Some said a ghost or ghosts roamed these parts, but no one had ever seen a ghost. Just heard...sounds. Word of mouth can put strange things in a scared person's mind. Also, the woods themselves can play tricks on you if you let it.

Leaves rustled as a swift early morning breeze awakened the woods. It was so early the sun was just barely up and struggling to force light through the huge trees and thick canopy. A small light bounced from tree to tree and swept over the ground. The light wasn't coming from the sun or a flashlight. It was actually the reflection from a pair of mirrored glasses worn by a man. Standing in a clearing was Lamont Huff. He had decided to look for clues around the crash Terry told them about. Never mind that Lamont wasn't a detective or trained to do this in any way. Never mind that the real police never found the body of the little girl supposedly lost in the woods. The real issue being ignored was the tragedy that happened nearly 25 years ago, but he still thought he could find something out there.

Hours passed and all he found was that he had gotten himself lost. At first he was angry. Why hadn't he found any clues? Any remains? Anything? After a while he accepted the fact that there was nothing to be found. As he wandered through the forest, Lamont stopped and took in the beauty of the woods. The sounds, the smells, the....the....what the hell was that? Lamont bent down and picked up a thick stick and moved toward something or other. As he got closer he could see that it was a leg. The leg of a person. A man. Could this be the body of the missing boy from the accident?! Never mind the fact that the accident was decades earlier and dead bodies don't grow. In his mind, this was the find he had come for.

Not until the leg moved did he realize that this wasn't the body of a child. It was a motherfucking grown-ass man, and he was alive!

With grunts and groans, the woodland man rose up and struggled to focus on the silhouette in front of him. "You sum bitch! What the hell you doing in my living room? You here to make old Jack move out his home in these woods? Gonna need more than some city breed weekend warrior to get me out of here, boy!"

Lamont was stunned first of all by this leaf-covered, big-bearded, dirty, zoo-smelling man that had magically come alive before his eyes, and Lamont quickly realized that the guy was also crazy as a dog with dentures. Stepping a little closer, sticking out his chest, and flexing, trying to seem as manly as possible even though he had peed himself a little, Lamont said to the guy, "Living room? You crazy old fuck. You do know there isn't a house or cabin nowhere near here. Your crazy ass was sleeping in the woods!"

"Just 'cause you don't see my home don't mean I ain't got none. City boy think he know everything just 'cause he buy pretty outdoor clothes and try to play Indiana Jones."

"Fuck you old man, and how you know I'm from the city?" Lamont yells.

"You dumbass. You smell like the city. That soap and strong damn cologne. Surprised those wild dogs aren't on your ass yet."

"What you know 'bout soap and cologne, old man? You smell like burnt ass out here."

"Old Jack ain't always been in the woods, boy. I smell like this to blend in with nature. Smell like the woods, the woods leave you alone," Jack answered, rising to his feet.

"Well, Jack! How long have you been homeless living out here? How do you survive?"

"Too many questions, city boy. Jack not homeless. My home is up in the trees. Away from four-legged hungry mouths. How long I been out here?" Jack took a long pause, then said, "Too long. Out here way too long!"

After a few more questions and half-ass answers, the two men went walking off together, headed to a huge tree. Jack pointed up toward the top. Lamont squinted and barely made out the shadowy image of a crude hut. A tree house basically. Jack unwrapped a homemade rope ladder from behind the tree, then they climbed up. In the tree house Jack actually had everything he needed to survive out there.

Sipping on a bottle of water in a makeshift swing chair, Lamont asked Jack if he was in the forest during the time of the accident. Jack got up and walked to the other side of the tiny tree house. Looking out of a little plexiglass window gazing into the woods like a flashback in the movies, Jack took a very long pause, then answered, "Yes. I didn't see the wreck, but I heard it. After coming down to check out the noise, I saw the car upside down and Vivian hanging out the window dead."

"Who is Vivian?" Lamont blurted out.

"The woman who was driving the car! The dead woman in the woods you just asked about! Keep up, concrete jungle monkey. I saw one of her kids laid out dead, not too far away from the car, with its body all bloody and broken up. Once the fuzz came..."

"Who the fuck is the fuzz, you crazy-ass old man?" Lamont said with a puzzled look on his face.

Rolling his eyes and sighing, Jack said, "The police, Johnny law, five-0, the pigs, the motherfucking fuzz, man. I'm a old schooler as the kids say today," As he slapped the wall with every example, Jack said, "Now let me finish. When the P O L I C E was out there I heard them say Vivian had put her youngest baby in the oven and turned it on, but I've known Viv for a long time, even before I left city life behind and came out here. Sometimes her and her husband would camp out here and leave me some of that good food with a note saying, 'Eat right, Mr. Foss.' By the way, Mr. Foss is me."

"I figured that out, Jack!"

"They were good people. I also heard her husband, Max, was found hanging from a tree. All that has to be bullshit, they were really good people and she loved her kids..." Jacks voice trailed off as tears came in his eyes...even after all these years.

With true concern, Lamont got up and put a hand on Jack's shoulder, then asked how many kids did they have? Jack said three. The youngest, found in the oven, who should have been around 4 or 5, and an older boy and girl. The boy about 7 and girl about 9. Terry said that he'd heard that the boy had wandered off and never was found.

"Boy! Bullshit! Well...I think that boy was dead...I saw a body close to his mom and car.

They never found his sister...hopefully the wild dogs didn't find her," Jack proclaimed, then let his voice soften as his gaze was occupied by the trees outside the window.

Chapter VI

Elizabeth Huff tapped her fingers on the steering wheel as she drove through the streets of the so-called downtown of this small country town. Every time she had to come into town, she would wish she was back in the actual city, living life to the fullest. Then the thought of losing Lamont to a reckless, foolish, compulsive act would simply tear her heart out. Before the move they even considered a new, private thrill trip that was being offered to wealthy extremists. A two-mile water-skiing trip down the Amazon through crocodile-infested water. As they were packing, the very real fact of possibly falling in and being catcn alive sent icy chills down Elizabeth's back. Then making Lamont picture her being torn apart by the crocs brought tears to his eyes. At that moment they decided to grow up in a sense and leave the wild life behind.

As she pulled up in front of the library, her phone rang. Glancing at the number, Liz spoke to herself out loud, but softly. "Sorry, Cindy. Our coffee date will have to wait for a few. Lamont needs me to do something first."

Lamont had asked Elizabeth to go do some research at the local library and try to dig up some kind, any kind, of information on the family that lived in the Tonners' home. Although they were not thrill-seekers any longer, Lamont had begun to consider himself and Elizabeth,, mainly himself, as amateur detectives. Lamont once found a neighbor's dog and found Liz's keys a couple times. So, he thought of himself as a detective. That's why he was in the woods somewhere and Liz was in town at the library doing a paper trail search.

It had been almost two hours of useless looking through internet sites, and Liz was beyond frustrated. Closing all open search pages, she leaned back in the chair and ran her fingers through her hair.

"To hell with this slow-ass computer, this ragged-ass town, and that fucking missing person, lost, dead or whatever family in the woods!" Liz murmured.

"Oh, you're looking for information on the Denton murder, missing family situation. That wouldn't be on that computer thing. Folks around here just tried to erase that out of our town's history all together," a soft older voice says somewhere behind Liz.

Spinning around, she saw an old woman with silver hair, smiling and leaning on a cart which was used more to help her stand up than to carry the books that were on it. At first Liz was startled, but after seeing this little old woman, all she could do was smile at her. She looked like someone's sweet grandmother. She should be somewhere making cookies. Not working in this library shuffling around.

"Yes ma'am. I was looking for some info on them. We live next door to their old home and have become friends with the new occupants. Recently the neighbor on the other side told all of us about a death in the house and possible crash and death of the rest of the family," Liz explained.

"It's great that someone has finally moved in. It's true a death happened there. I was a younger woman back then when it happened. A spring bird of 65 or so. I'm 95 now," the small librarian said, giggling.

"Oh honey, you don't look nowhere near that old."

"You sweet child you! I love you to pieces for that. I'm old, but Father Time has been kind to me. So, what exactly did you need to know about them?"

"Well...after the story we were told, my husband and I became fascinated with them and what happened to them. My crazy husband is out in the woods right now trying to find some clues."

"30 years later, honey?"

Laughing, Liz said she knew it would be impossible, but her husband was headstrong and stubborn once his mind was set on something. So, if she could show her any old newspaper clippings or knew any rumors, it would be greatly appreciated and help settle down her husband's amateur mystery-solving itch. The little woman took her hand

and led her to the newspaper area. The librarian told her she could look for another two hours and not find what she wanted, but if she could spare time and patience by sitting with an old woman, she could tell her all she knew. Patting the old woman's fragile hand and smiling, Liz told her to lead the way to a comfortable seat.

After the two women found a pair of chairs, the librarian named Ms. Shaze began to tell her version of the horrible murders that supposedly happened in the Tonners' home. Her story was similar to Terry's story. The husband was found dead in the home along with a neighbor. A child's life was almost taken. Rumors around town were that the husband tried to do something to the baby, but Ms. Shaze said she didn't believe that. Mr.

Denton loved his kids. The neighbors once said he charged a coyote that was stalking the baby outside. So, for him to harm her is pure snot dogs. Liz held in her laugh when she heard "snot dogs," but Ms. Shaze didn't curse.

"So, was the baby in the car with Mrs. Denton when it crashed in the woods?" Liz asked as she sipped on a hot tea that was given to her.

"Sadly, yes she was. Along with the other two, we think."

"Think?" Liz said.

"Yes. Think. The mother's body was found burnt, still in the car, and the baby was also burnt. Poor child, but only one body was found outside the car. The kids must have run out on fire, so they didn't get burned alive. One body was found close to the car. We figured the other body was dragged off by an animal in the woods," Ms. Shaze answered with tears in her eyes.

"So, the boy's body was never found, and the girl's remains are still yet to be found?" Liz asked before taking another sip of the drink.

"Who said it was the girl's body missing? Yes...a body is missing, but only the police report says it was the girl, Candice. I'm guessing it just made it easier to say something took the dead child away. If that was so true, why has no human child remains ever been found? Even after all the years gone by, and search parties. NOTHING!!" The librarian said while leaning in close to Liz so no nosey ear could hear.

The two women continued to drink tea and discuss the Dentons until a very curious thing was mentioned. That the first person on site was an Officer Bock. Terry Bock. During his telling of the story, he forgot to mention he was actually there. Liz thought, "Wait until Lamont gets this info, he's going to lose his shit! Looks like this little field trip wasn't a waste after all!"

Chapter VII

As the night began to swallow the area, Patrick and his son Clint came into the house dirty and sweaty. Patrick was mostly sweaty from his work of chopping wood for the fireplace inside, while Clint was mostly dirty from being a small boy outside. Cindy was in the kitchen fixing dinner for them and thinking of dessert later with her husband. Being preoccupied with cooking, she didn't notice the figure coming up behind her until it cast a shadow on the wall in front of her. Cindy jumped and spun around with a large, very sharp knife in hand. Patrick fell back and said, "Holy shit, Cin! It's just me!"

Dropping the blade, she covered her mouth while quietly saying, "Oh my god!" And reaching out to hug him. Holding him tight, she kept apologizing and telling him how sorry she was. After gathering himself, he reassured her he was OK and that the mistake was his. He knew how on edge she had been for a while now, and he just didn't think when he came up behind her.

Kissing Patrick's cheek, she followed him upstairs and ran bath water for Clint while Patrick chased him around trying to get those dirty clothes off. After Clint's bath and a good tub scrubbing he ran water for his shower. He yelled down the stairs that he would be down for dinner right after his shower. While he soaped his body and face, a cold shiver ran down his back. The water was very hot as all the steam in the bathroom could show. Yet the coldness down the back still was there, and through the steam he kind of, sort of, saw a figure right outside the shower door. He tried to focus his vision by squinting his eyes, but immediately assumed it was Cindy coming to join him. Then the...whatever it was...rushed at him and pushed the glass door in on him. As he fell down in the tub, the glass door shattered against the wall, throwing large pieces of glass on him. With the mixture of water, steam, and glass in his face and all over him, he couldn't see who pushed the door. As he flopped around his mind went right to Cin and the visions she said she was seeing. As soon as it came in his mind, he pushed it out, figuring it must have been Clint that had fallen against the door.

While he struggled to get out of the tub, he yelled for his wife because he still had glass in his face and could feel glass on the floor. She came around the corner asking, "What's wrong?" and saw Patrick wet, bleeding, and halfway in the tub and on the floor.

Cindy cried out, "Oh, my God," and ran to Patrick, pulling the door off of him. She cleaned his face very carefully with a towel that hung on a rack on the bathroom wall. Clint had come around the corner too, holding his favorite stuffed bear and asking what was wrong with his daddy. She asked Clint if he had been in there and accidentally fallen against the door. He said no and that he had been in his room playing with his bear, Mr. Rags.

Patrick sat up and looked at Clint. In his mind, he was sizing Clint up to the figure that was in there. Clint was way too small. So, Patrick convinced himself that something that was already in there made a shadow, and the door had just come off track on its own. He couldn't possibly let Cindy think her paranoia was happening to him too. Cleaning up the glass off the floor and making sure there was no glass left in his face they went down and ate dinner. Afterward, they put Clint to bed, and they called it a night too.

As they rested in bed, she laid her head on his chest. He felt his chest getting wet, so he looked down at her. Lifting her head, he saw tears running down her face. Looking back up at him, she cried even more.

"I have been a terrible wife to you, Pat. I'm losing my mind, stressing you out, and most importantly, I can't give you a child,." Cindy said as she continued to cry.

"Cin, don't talk like that. You have been....you ARE a great wife. The stress of the move and very different surroundings are the cause of you thinking you're seeing things, so don't blame yourself."

"I know, I know, but it's not just all of this. This is just what's going on now. On top of all my issues here, my biggest failure is that I can't give you the family you want."

"What are you talking about? We have a great family. You, me, and Clint," Patrick said with a puzzled look.

"Yes. Yes, we do, but Clint is your son. I love him just as much as if I gave birth to him myself, but I didn't. I want to give you life from my own body to go along with Clint. I am so sorry that I can't. By now you are probably wishing you never married..."

Right then he put his finger up to her lip to quiet her. He moved around to position himself directly in front of her to look right in her the face. Taking her hand ever so gently, Patrick pulled it to his chest and told her he had never regretted marrying her. She had previously told him she couldn't have kids due to a childhood incident, and he loved her no less. He never pressured her to explain the issue. She would tell him when and if she felt comfortable enough. She tried a couple times, but their love had grown so much it no longer mattered to him.

"Cin! Listen to me right now and don't you ever forget it. I loved you then. I love you now, and I will love you until time is forgotten. You two are the most important things to me. You two are my life. If we were somehow blessed to have a baby, that would be great. If not, I am perfectly fine with our family right here. You may not be his birth mother, but that kid loves you as if you were. And you know why? Because you love him. Because you love us. Now I'm going to need you to stop beating yourself up."

With a smile he glanced over to an object on the dresser. "If you wanna get beat, you can always grab that belt over there, turn off the lights, and bend over."

Drying her eyes, she leaned forward and kissed him, then told him, "You so nasty."

Chapter VIII

The next day, Terry was finishing up cutting the Tonners' yard. He'd offered to do it because Patrick had been working long hours and just didn't have time. In truth Terry wanted to cut the yard because he wanted every second he could get riding his new lawnmower. It was true that Mr. Bock was known to help out just about anyone in town that he could because he was retired and had time. Mainly due to the fact he just wanted to be and feel useful. Since his retirement from the force, Terry Bock was a shell of himself. On the outside, he was a joking, fun-loving man, but on the inside he....he just wasn't himself. On the force he had a purpose every day. Protect and serve the citizens in the town. Now it felt like he was just an old man waiting for death's call. Sure, Samantha needed her husband, but she had a life before him and she could manage without him after some time. So, wherever and whenever he was asked to help, after some clowning around, Terry was there.

The yard was done, and it was payment time. So, Terry sat on his lawnmower waiting for Cindy to come out. She finally came with a tray and a pitcher with 2 glasses. She filled the two glasses and handed him one.

"Here is your payment. One cold glass of homemade lemonade."

He reached down and took the glass. After a slow sip a huge smile came across his face.

"Paid in full with the best money there is. Thank you, Cindy."

"All this yard and all you wanted was a pitcher of lemonade? You sure I can't actually pay you?" Cindy asked, putting her hand in her pocket for some cash.

Just then, Lamont and Elizabeth came across the yard on mountain bikes with dust flying up behind them. Cindy and Terry turned toward the two and looked back at each other and giggled.

"I wonder what's got ants in their pants today," Terry said before downing another glass.

Lamont and Elizabeth rolled to a stop, kicking up a dust and leaf cloud that covered Terry and Cindy. After a few curses from Terry and coughs from Cindy, the two bikers apologized and immediately started in on Terry. They told him they knew he was one of the first officers at the scene of the accident. Terry slowly put his glass down to his side and dropped his head with a sigh.

"Who told you this?"

"I was told by the little librarian in town. She said you were one of the first at the crash, and only three bodies were found. The mother, her baby, and a child. The other child's body was never found" Elizabeth said.

Then Lamont spoke up and said, "And I saw the burnt car shell. Plus, I talked to a man that lives out there in the woods."

"Man living in the woods? What do you mean he lives there?" Cindy asked with shock in her tone.

"Well, hell. That explains a lot." Terry said while pouring another glass of lemonade.

"Who is he, Terry?"

"Jack Foss. We call him Lumber Jack. He has been out there longer than some of those trees. Jack used to be in business in the city with a Harold Donovan. They started a talent agency called The Donovan Foss Agency, but it didn't really take off at first. Until Harold's wife came in with them. Vicki, she recommended they work with models only. The business began to gain momentum, but at the same time, Jack's son and wife were killed. With his mind obviously not in the business anymore, he called in a favor to an old friend, Jack Adams, to come take his place with the Donovans. They all agreed he should take some time away. He moved here to clear his head, but didn't find real peace till he started camping out. So, he decided to just stay out there."

"Sounds like a crazy man living in the woods like that," Cindy said.

Looking over at her, Terry replied, "Jack is far from crazy. A little different, but not crazy."

"What did you see, or know, that you're not telling everyone?!" Elizabeth asked while touching Terry's hand.

"Know for sure....nothing…but while searching I heard a car's brakes slam on, then the sound of I guess the same car driving away real fast a few seconds later. I told my captain, but with not seeing the car he just dismissed it as a nosey passerby. In my opinion, that car has something to do with that other child not being found."

Chapter IX

Three days passed, and the group of men were back together doing their normal thing. Drinking beer, grilling food, and talking shit. Cindy had told Patrick about the information Lamont and Elizabeth brought to her and Terry. The three men also discussed Lumber Jack living in the woods. Terry had to reassure the other men that although he may have come off strange and very odd, Jack was harmless. Terry called him a "paper tiger," saying his roar was much worse than his bite. If they wanted he could take them directly to where he stayed out there. Turning up a beer, Patrick firmly said, "No thank you." Lamont considered it, then thought of the argument that would come afterward from Liz. So, he also declined.

"Where is Cindy today? I usually see her and Clint out running around in the field during the day," Terry asks before pulling a flask out of his back pocket.

"What's in the flask, Terry?"

"Good ol' Kentucky bourbon, Lamont. Kids need milk, and adults need bourbon."

Patrick laughed, then told the men that Cindy had been having bad headaches lately. He didn't mention she had also been seeing a shadow man in the house and out in the yard. Bad enough they were there when she thought Clint was in the oven. "She has gone to see her doctor in the city to get her prescription for her migraines. Regular pills aren't strong enough."

"That's a damn shame, hope she gets some help with that," Lamont said with genuine concern.

Terry asks, "Why didn't you go with her, she isn't nervous going by herself?"

"Matter of fact, I have never been with her to see him. Said he has been her doc since she was a child, and he was almost like family or close enough to it."

"Shit! I wish Sam would let me go see a doctor alone. Hell, I barely get to come out with you guys without her checking on me." Then he took another taste from the flask.

Patrick and Lamont laughed and said, "Wonder why!?" Terry grinned and looked at the flask and said, "I see what you mean. On a serious note, I think you should go up there and see that doctor for yourself. Women are just as bad as us, but better at it. They won't tell you anything they don't want you to know."

"That's true. I think I will make a trip to see him tomorrow. I am due a half-day anyway. I'll just tell Cin when I get back."

The men all clinked their drinks together and said, "Here's to Cindy's doc, and her feeling better."

Chapter X

7:00 p.m.

A few days later, Cindy spent time at home, doing this and that, trying to keep herself busy while Patrick was at work. Clint played in his room with some action figures. His dad only let him play with actual toys because he thought video games hampered imagination. To Patrick, all the great doers in the world were successful because they used their imagination to get where they were in life. While Clint was off on some distant world fighting midget monkeys, AKA his pillows and giant action figures, Cindy was cleaning up in the den when she felt a cold chill run up her back. Looking over her shoulder she saw the shadow figure off in the distance staring at her. This time, the shadow had eyes that burned ruby red. Then the…thing…moved closer to her. She was frozen in place with fear. Then it spoke in a roar, "I AM HERE!" Then it grew and ran at her. The room turned pitch black, and it grabbed her and pushed her to the ground. Pinned to the floor, Cindy tried to scream, but the thing seemed to take her breath.

"LET ME IN!"

As Cindy began to black out, sound finally came from her mouth. "What are you?!?!" Then she let off a blood chilling scream.

8:15 p.m.

Terry was on the way home, passing the Tonners' home, when he heard a faint sound. Definitely not an animal, but maybe a person? Out of curiosity and willingness to be a good neighbor, he thought he would just pull up in the driveway and have a look around. Getting out, he told his passenger to sit tight, and he would be right back.

Walking through the yard he saw....something....crouched down between two bushes. Not really being scared, but not being a complete fool either, Terry snapped a branch off a tree and moved closer to the thing very slowly. "Whatever the hell you are, come out from behind there!" Then a small figure ran out and wrapped around his legs. Looking down, he dropped the branch. "Oh my God! Clint, why are you outside alone!?"

"I was scared. It got Cindy, then it came for me."

Being very impatient, the passenger in Terry's truck got out and lit up a cigarette. Through the smoke, a pair of eyes glared at him. Focusing on the eyes, he dropped ashes on himself and burned a small hole in his shirt. Looking down he didn't see the brick that was flying at him. Catching him right in the head he stumbled back against the truck. A blade was forced into his chest. Dazed and now stabbed, he managed to push the attacker back so he could make a run for it. With blurred vision and a burning pain in his chest, the man ran farther into the yard and farther into the darkness. A sound of steps coming up fast behind him caused the guy to turn slightly, then get caught in the rope swing. A huge branch to the face took his sight. The rope was looped around his neck and hoisted in the air. In pain, bleeding, head concussion possibly, and now choking to death. Finally, the night was still again, except for the lifeless body swinging in the night air.

Terry held Clint's hand and moved quickly to the house. He asked how he got out and what exactly it was that got Cindy, and what did it do to her? The boy tried explaining while they went through the yard going to the side door. Terry never got a clear understanding of what Clint was trying to tell him because he was so young and scared. Once inside, Terry kept the child behind him and looked through the house. No lights were on, and furniture was knocked around. Probably from the person chasing Clint. In the kitchen food was burning on the stove,and the sink had overrun with water. Also, a butcher knife was missing from the block. Just then he remembered his passenger in the truck and went back out. Outside at the truck, no one was there. Something in the distance caught his eye. Something in the trees. Clint stayed close to him as they inched closer. Terry's mouth flew open as the image came into focus. With terror and great sadness, he groaned, "Oh no, poor Jack! Why didn't you stay in the truck?"

7:20 pm

In town, Patrick went to an address he had for Cindy's doctor. He left work early just for this, but didn't tell her. He didn't want her to try and discourage him from going like usual.

He wanted information on her condition because he really wanted to help her. The place where he went was empty, abandoned. Confused now, Patrick started asking around about the doctor. Most waved him off, and some gave no response at all and simply walked away. Finally, one old man told him an address where the doctor had been for the last 10 years.

8:00 pm

Pulling up to this new address, Patrick got out of his truck very slowly looking at the sign overhead. Saying to himself, "What the fuck," he looked at the address then the sign again. Both matched. The sign said "cemetery." In utter shock, he walked on into the cemetery. Looking around he saw a groundskeeper tending to fresh flowers around a grave.

"Sir! Excuse me, but can you tell me if a Doctor Chris Hoss is buried here?"

"Sure is. He is right over there, follow me. Were you a former patient of the doc's?"

"No sir. My wife is...was."

"Doc doesn't get many visitors, considering his past and having his license revoked."

"His past? License revoked! When did all this take place? My wife has been coming to see Dr. Hoss since she was a pre-teen, and she just had an appointment not long ago."

Looking at Patrick up and down, the keeper says, "How could she have been a patient of Hoss and seen him? He has been there in the ground for the last 10 years. Unless you married an insect or rodent, there is no way she has been a patient."

"Wait, wait, wait! My wife has been saying she has been seeing him for the last...she has prescription pills...this fucker is dead!"

"That's right. Old Doc Hoss was poisoned by his last nurse. She found out some crazy shit about him and things he did. No one believed her 'cause to the public he was the good doctor. In reality he was a real-life Dr. Frankenstein."

"I'm guessing she is buried around here too?"

"No, sir. She is still in jail for murder. Nurse Straw. Linda Straw, I believe. Yep, the lady is still locked up. Go see her. She got more dirt on Hoss than I do." Then the groundskeeper erupted in laughter. Patrick walked away still confused, but hopeful that this Nurse Straw could clear up this mess.

"Oh, I forgot. This lady comes by every now and then to sit and talk over the grave for a few minutes, then leaves."

Patrick came back and took out his phone to show him a picture of Cindy.

"Yep. That's the woman. A bit touched if you ask me. Your wife, huh? Better you than me buddy."

Back in the car, Patrick typed "state prison" into his G.P.S., then took off.

8:42 pm

Inside the state prison, Patrick waited at a window for inmate Linda Straw to be brought in. As he sat, his mind tried to grasp the fact that his wife could possibly have been lying to him their whole relationship. Was it true that she was adopted as a young child, and they died when she was 18? That she was seeing a doctor at all, never mind seeing a dead doctor? Or could it be that the groundskeeper was full of shit? One truth was clear. The man she said was her doctor was a cold skeleton with 6 feet of dirt on his chest. Then a door in back, behind the bullet proof glass, opened. A little woman wearing cuffs was brought in, and she sat down in front of him. Picking up the phone on her side, she stared at Patrick and asked, "What the hell you want?"

Through his phone he answered, "All I want is information about Dr. Chris Hoss. I was told you used to work for him."

"That's right, I did. And before you ask, yes, I did kill him!"

"Why, did he do something to you?"

"No. Not to me, but that little boy. After I found out what he did, I just snapped. Oh, I didn't know for years upon years, but I did find out."

"He was a child molester?"

"No, all I knew was that he was raising a young girl he said he adopted. Come to find out that was all bullshit."

They conversed for a few minutes more. Then Patrick got some news that left him speechless. Without a "thank you" or a "good-bye," he slowly got up and left. Outside he stopped at his truck and damn near passed out. He couldn't believe what he'd just heard. No fucking way. Gathering himself, he got into his truck, pulled a small bottle out from the glove box, and downed the dark, harsh liquid. His cell rang. "Not now, oh, hello, Terry. You got who with you? Holy shit...hold on, hold on, I'm losing you. You were passing my place and what? A scream? What.....don't go back in to my place. Go home...Terry...can you hear me...Terry!!!!!! Just go home!!!!"

Chapter XI

After a call from Patrick, Lamont told Elizabeth that he needed to run down to Pat and Cin's house to check on things. Once there, he parked behind Terry's truck, pulled out a flashlight from the glove box, and looked around the yard. In the house he was acting like a badass in front of his wife, but now that he was out there by himself, Lamont's bravery was more than a little shaky. He was walking slowly and jumping at every sound. Noticing something moving through the field in the distance, he froze, and instead of walking up to whatever it was, he picked up a large rock and threw it. Speaking softly to himself, he says, "Fuck that checking mysterious shit out in the dark, that's movie shit." So, he pointed the light where the rock went, and waited. Nothing. Thinking it may have been nothing but a possum or raccoon, he moved on ahead. Suddenly, a fully grown deer jumped right in front of him. Falling back, he bumped into something.

"What the hell is that?" Trying to focus in the dark, he said, "That damn tire swing of Clint's." He aimed the flashlight so he could kick it. Then he saw the body swinging. Horror turned into shock after he noticed who it was. "Jack! Oh shit!" Then sadness set in, because even though he didn't really know Jack, he liked him. "Damn...poor Jack. Who did this to you?"

His mind immediately went to Terry, Cindy, and little Clint. With that, his bravery finally showed up because of the concern for his friends. So, he started to yell, "Where are you?" and ran toward the house.

Inside, Terry held Clint as they hid in the back of a large walk-in closet that no one knew of but Clint. He fell into it while playing hide-and-seek with Cindy. It was behind a false panel in the hallway. While they tried to stay as quiet as possible, Terry tried texting his wife. Somehow, somewhere, he had broken his phone.

With a whisper, he asked Clint, "Where is Cindy? Where was she last?" Before Clint could answer, they heard someone yelling.

"Where is everyone? Cindy? Clint? Terry? Anyone? Where the hell are you?"

Terry pushed open the secret door, and Lamont dropped his flashlight and probably peed himself a little. Seeing old Terry, and seeing that Terry had Clint, made Lamont feel much better. Now if he only knew where Cindy was.

"Clint, where is Cindy?" Lamont asked, bending down to hug the kid. Clint looked up at Terry, then back to Lamont. He never answered, just pointed to a pitch-black hallway. The two men turned in unison and saw a figure standing in the darkness staring at them. They figured it was Cindy, confused at who they were.

Terry spoke up and said, "Cindy, it's us. It's Terry, Lamont, and Clint. Are you OK?"

From the darkness knives came flying at them. A couple hit the wall, and one hit Lamont in the chest. "What the FUCK! Cindy, stop!"

From behind them, shots came whizzing overhead. They took cover again as the bullets screamed by. Clint got up first and ran to the doorway where the shots came from. He latched himself to the shooter's leg and held on tight. The two men on the floor looked up and first saw a large handgun over their heads, then saw that it was Patrick holding the gun. He told them to get up and get out because they were in more danger than they knew. "That fucker there is not

Cindy! You hear me motherfucker? I know who the hell you are!"

"Is that the guy who killed poor Jack out there? Did he do something to Cindy?"

"Killed Jack, yes, hurt Cindy, no! There is no Cindy, there never was!"

More than confused, the men got up and stared at Patrick. Terry asked first, "What do you mean, there never was a Cindy?" Lamont sounded off next, saying, "Are you crazy? We know Cindy!"

While the men were distracted, the person charged them, knocking the whole group down. Then Clint was grabbed and pulled off into the dark. In the fall, Patrick dropped his gun but saw Clint being taken. So, he got up and ran off after them into the darkness. The other two guys got up then ran the same way after they heard Clint screaming. They didn't worry about the person who took the child or the dark hallway. They just knew they needed to go. Lamont had pulled the knife out of the right side of his chest and now had it in hand as his own weapon. Terry was running ahead of him with weapon in hand.

The hall led to the kitchen, which had a little light from the moon coming in through the window. In horror, they saw Patrick lying in the doorway bleeding from the head. Over in the corner they saw the oven door open, and the inside was red hot. Then they saw the figure dragging Clint over to it with the intent of throwing him in.

"No! Don't do it!" Terry yelled.

Lamont took the knife and threw it, hitting the person with the handle part. Patrick, while lying on the ground, reached up and took the weapon out of Terry's hand and started shooting at the person again, hitting them in the leg and forcing them to let Clint go and run out of the room.

Picking Patrick up, Lamont asked "Who was that? Where the fuck is Cindy?"

"That was Cindy! Or the person that's been calling himself Cindy. That actually was Christopher Denton!"

"Christopher Denton? He died years ago in the woods with his family!"

"No. Actually, he didn't. I'll tell you after we get this asshole. Lamont, you good to go?"

"I'm good. Let's get the motherfucker."

With Terry being the oldest, he was asked to stay behind to keep an eye on Clint. Wanting to help catch the man that hung Jack, he reluctantly agreed to stay. Patrick and Lamont took off out the door. In the distance, they could see a figure leaning against something. As the figure became more visible in the moonlight, they could see Christopher wasn't alone. He had poor Samantha in a chokehold. As the two men tried to overtake him, Christopher started to tighten his clutch around her neck. With tears rolling down her face, she pleaded and begged for help.

Patrick took a step forward and spoke to Christopher. "Chris, please let her go. I know. I know everything that you have been through and what was done to you. I know Dr. Hoss found you on the side of the road after your family car crashed. He found a young boy. A boy who tried to put his baby sister in the oven and killed his father. Also tried to kill his mother and sister while she drove. He took you and changed you. Changed you in a sex change operation. He had always wanted a girl, so he told everyone he adopted you and raised you. No longer Christopher, now Cindy. He kept you drugged to keep the memory of Chris away, and it worked until you moved back into your old house. You weren't seeing visions. You were having memory flashbacks. The shadow that pushed the glass in on me was you."

"Cindy was a fucking....is a fucking man?! You were fucking a former man, dude?!"

"Not helping, Lamont."

"Yes. Dr. Hoss raised me and loved me as a daughter and a lover. Until that bitch nurse saw me sucking his dick. Then she killed him because she believed he was abusing me. So, I set her straight after I had her arrested. Sometime later I met you. I did love you Patrick, but now since I remember everything, I must kill you all and write myself another prescription for pills so I can forget all this and start over. First this old bitch dies first." With a twist of the neck, Chris took Samantha's life.

As her body fell, a loud, "NO!!!" comes out of the darkness, followed by a flash of fire. Then more flashes that sent Chris flying back with several on-target gunshots. Terry emerged in the moonlight and dropped the smoking gun to the ground. He fell to his knees next to his wife's lifeless body, then picked her up and took her to his truck to head home. Patrick picked up the gun, stood over Christopher's body, and emptied the clip in his chest. Terry rode past, stopped and said, "Clint is in his hiding spot in the wall, just go in and call him." As he drove off, he made sure to have at least two of his wheels roll over that body. Lamont put his hand on Pat's shoulder and led him back to the house.

Chapter XII

The police came and went, and explanations and accounts were given. Jack's body was removed from the tree, and Samantha's body was collected from her home. Lamont went home to Elizabeth a nervous wreck, promising never to leave her side and also making jokes about if she was born a man or woman tell him now. Patrick comforted Clint and tried to explain why Cindy came after him, what she...he...really was, and why they were alone now and would be moving back to the city. Terry...poor Terry...sat at home trying to wrap his mind around the fact that the love of his life was gone.

Once before, this quiet little town in the country had been stirred up by terrible happenings. It's sad that horror had to come from and revolve around this home.....again. Soon the home will be empty again, and there is a tree house out there in the woods that will no longer have its watchman there to look after the woods.

Now the area rests. Rests and sleeps until the next home, the next family, the next tragedy all stir and awaken more Forgotten Lies...

The End

Michael Young

www.ingramcontent.com/pod-product-compliance
Lightning Source LLC
Chambersburg PA
CBHW071132250626
47159CB00006B/2212